Thanks for Thanksgiving

by **Julie Markes**

illustrated by **Doris Barrette**

HARPERCOLLINSPUBLISHERS

Thanks for Thanksgiving
Text copyright © 2004 by Julie Markes
Illustrations copyright © 2004 by Doris Barrette
Manufactured in China.
All rights reserved.
For information address HarperCollins Children's Books, a division of
HarperCollins Publishers, 195 Broadway, New York, NY 10007.
www.harpercollinschildrens.com

Library of Congress Cataloging-in-Publication Data
Markes, Julie.
Thanks for Thanksgiving / by Julie Markes ; illustrated by Doris Barrette.—
1st ed.
p.   cm.
Summary: At Thanksgiving time, children express their gratitude for people
and things in their lives.
ISBN 978-0-06-051096-1 (trade bdg.) — ISBN 978-0-06-051098-5 (pbk.)
[1. Thanksgiving Day—Fiction. 2. Gratitude—Fiction. 3. Stories in rhyme.]
I. Barrette, Doris, ill. II. Title.
PZ8.3.M391445 Th 2004   [E]—dc21   2002153420
CIP   AC

Typography by Stephanie Bart-Horvath
❖
First Edition
20 SCP 20 19 18 17

To my amazing mother, Diana,
for whom I am very thankful.
—J.M.

To my parents, Cécile and Gérald.
—D.B.

Thanks for Thanksgiving,
for turkey and pie.

Thank you for fall
and gold leaves floating by.

Thank you for school—
I love to feel smart!

Thank you for music
and dancing and art.

Thank you for play dates,
for swings and for slides.

Thank you for hopscotch
and piggyback rides.

Thanks for sweet puppies
and soft, furry cats.

Thank you for dress-up,
red shoes and big hats.